Because You Care For Beany Bear

Enjoy interacting in Beany Bear's Adventures.

Counting, Caring and Searching, with your help.

ISBN 978-0-9869229-5-4 (reading book)
ISBN 978-0-9869229-6-1 (colouring book)

Edited by Mary Graves
Typeset by Iryna Spica, SpicaBookDesign

Printed and bound in Canada
by Mitchell Press, Burnaby, BC

Other books by Christine Logan are:

To Touch Your Heart
ISBN 978-0-9869229-0-9

My Heart is Yours
ISBN 978-0-9869229-2-3

Special Tribute to Mothers Everywhere
(Co-Author to Gord Baird)
ISBN 978-0-9869229-1-6

Suppose
ISBN 978-1-5255-2070-9

Dedicated to all grandchildren everywhere

Inspired by
My handsome grandson, Kieran
Born on September 4, 2011.

Whose own nickname was
Baby Bean!

Thank you, Kieran

My heart-felt thanks and appreciation for all the time
and hard work from
Gayatri Ray from Bigmonky Creations (Fiverr)

Table of Contents

Because You Care 5

A Surprise For Beany. 13

Beany Bear's New Friends. 19

Andy the Spider 29

Beany Bear Meets His Mate 37

Our Thankful Bear 45

Because You Care

Beany bear is a caring bear.
He's black and hairy but never scary.

He searches for food,
he searches for friends.
His love for you never ends.

Beany bear needs all your help.
His eyesight is poor and so is his luck.

Find the berries, show him where.
Let Beany know how much you care.

7

Beany's nose smells very well.
He spies a bee's nest next to a well.

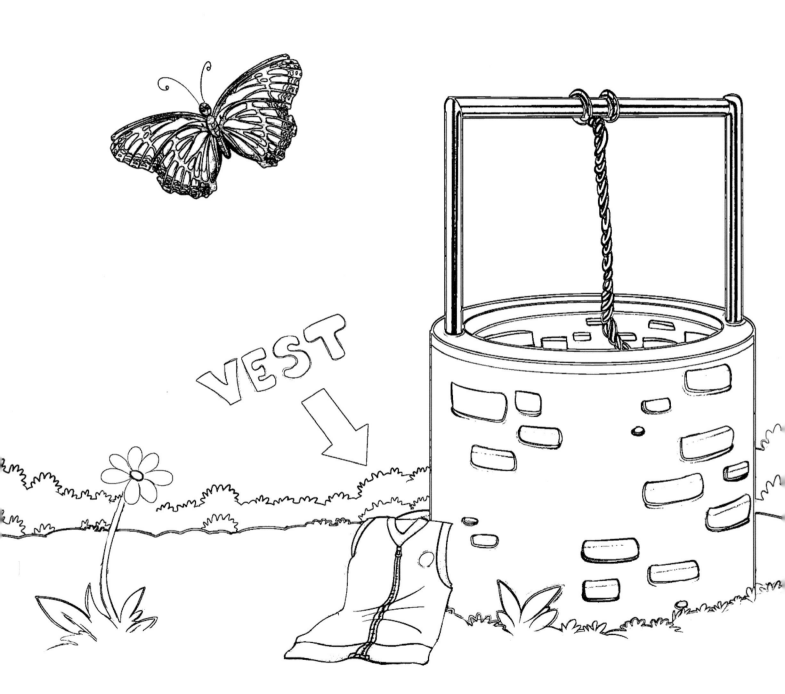

VEST

His hairy fur is very thick.
If he's not careful, the honey will stick.

A vest will save his hairy back and
keep him safe from a bee on bear attack.
Find the vest, help Beany out.
He'll do the rest,
then "HOORAY", we'll shout!

Full and fed, because you helped out.
Our friendly bear is nice and stout.

One last thing, before you go.
Find his cave and let Beany know . . .

It's time to sleep, to hibernate.
Until next year, it's getting late.

Say "Goodnight" to Beany bear.
He loves you and thanks you
because you care.

11

12

A Surprise For Beany

Beany awakes from a very long nap,
happily surprised to find a new friend....
Asleep in his lap!

Beany is happy,
the start to his spring
has brought him a friend.

He feels like a king.

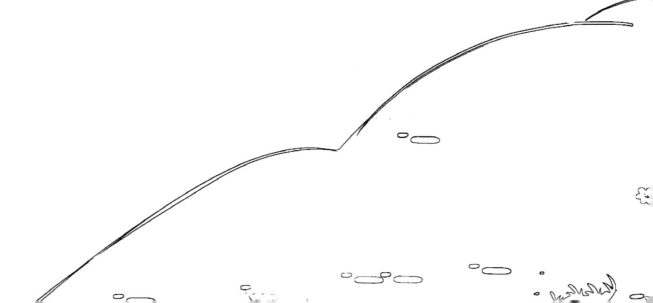

Her name is Sherma.
She loves to hum tunes.

Beany joins in as they search
for their food.

Find and count
(4 bugs and 12 berries)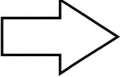

Full and content
because YOU were a part of the plan,
Beany and Sherma ate all that they can.

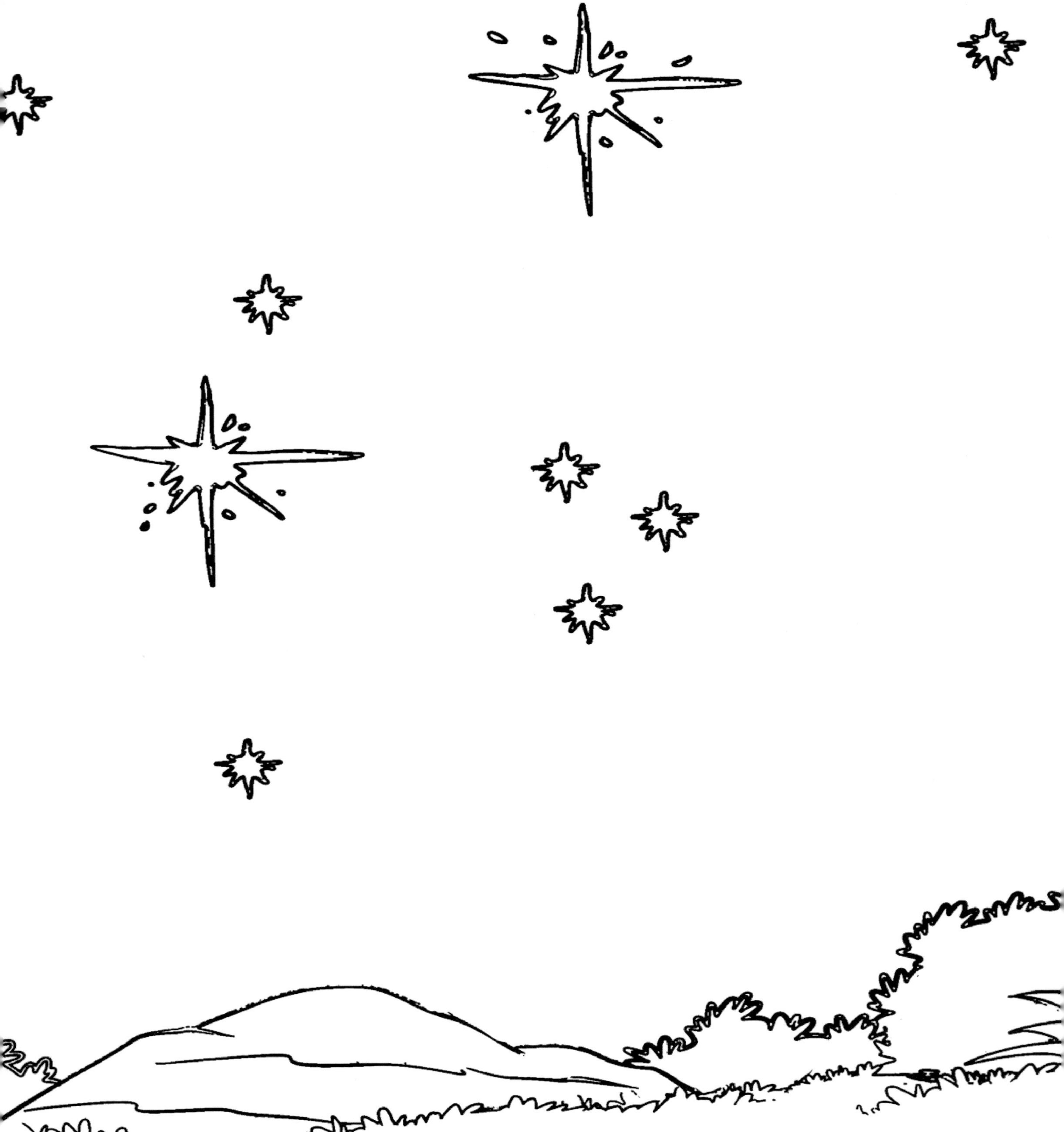

Beany Bear's New Friends

Beany and Sherma head back
to the cave before dark.

Oh oh, it's too late! They've lost
their way AND they've heard a bark!

BARK

BARK

Suddenly, as they turn around,
they bump into a _____?
All spotted in brown (YES! A puppy).

His name is Yoshi. He's shaking and scared.
Thankfully, Beany and Sherma remembered their way,
and told the puppy, "You don't have to stay.
Come with us, we'll keep you safe in the night.
We're sorry we gave you such a fright."

BEANY'S CAVE

Home to Beany's cave at last,
the three new friends fell
asleep so fast.

21

Beany, Yoshi and Sherma play most of the day.

Humming tunes along the way.
Jumping rope with what they can,
they have no idea they're about
to get a helping hand.

A colorful bunny spies their fun.
On the look-out for a skipping rope,
he'll search and run.

His name is Teeny. With your help,
he's found a skip-rope to bring back to Sherma,
Yoshi and Beany.

Help guide Teeny back,
he'll be the save of the day.
To Beany, Yoshi and Sherma so they
ALL can play!

Playing hard and skipping for hours,
leaves our four friends tuckered

So they stop to pick flowers.

Flowers to put in a jar, once they're home
it won't be long, it's not that far.

Ten minutes or so is what it will take,
to reach Beany's home near the lake.

Exhausted and thankful with your help
and Teeny's,
their day is complete until your next visit
with Beany.

Beany requests his friends stay the night.
It's dark out and safer, so they, "Alright."

Beany tells his friends, "Sweet dreams" and
they tell him, "Good night."

They're all tucked in, content and happy
until the morning light.

It seems whenever Beany wakes,
another friend he makes.

This little friend, in the dark of night,
kept his distance and out of sight.

Until he sees a fly over there,
crawling near our sleeping bear.

With one swift leap and a little jump,
this hungry spider now is plump. Mmm.

Late in the evening, our Beany found
this tiny spider crawling around.

Beany said, "Are you alright?"
The spider replied,
"Yes, I just fed through the night."

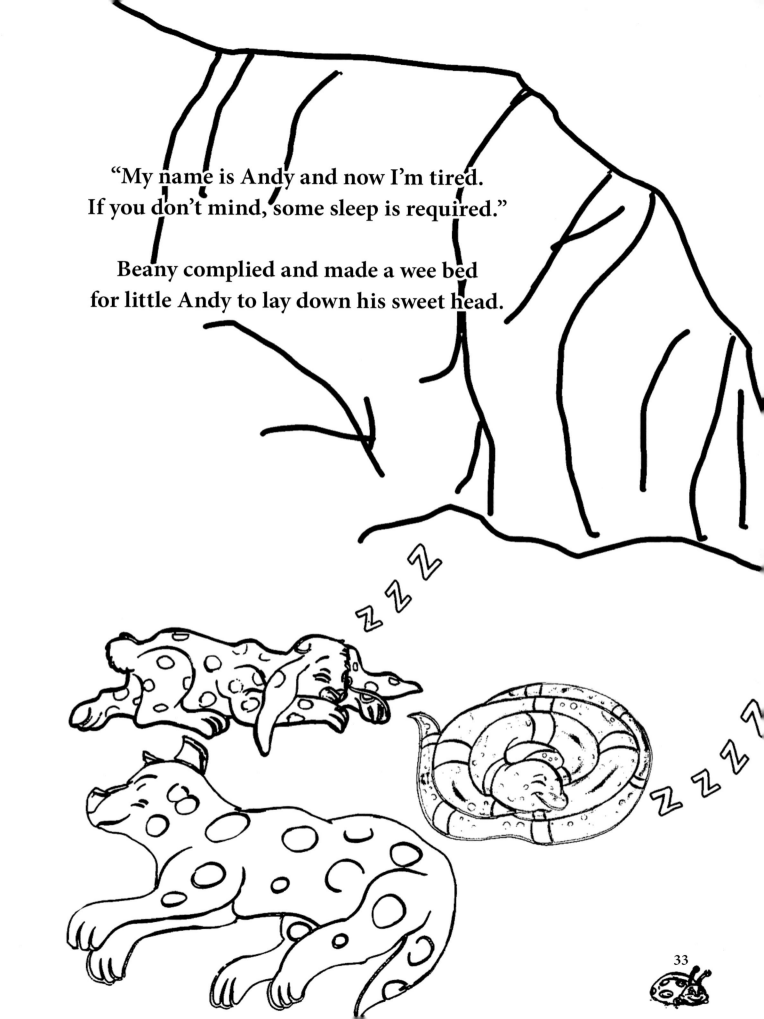

"My name is Andy and now I'm tired.
If you don't mind, some sleep is required."

Beany complied and made a wee bed
for little Andy to lay down his sweet head.

Awake at last,
and ready to play,
they all get acquainted
for a brand new day.

34

Beany Bear Meets His Mate

Another year of hibernation.
Awake again to seek the nation.

Beany's grown and needs a wife,
with your keen eyesight and all your help,
Beany will find the mate of his life.

As Beany looks for the love of his life,
his friends are nearby with good advice.

Sherma talks in Beany's ear,
"There's a creek nearby with plump fish from thissss year."

How many fish can you count?
How many bears do you see?
With your help and all that's there,
there's bound to be love
for our Beany bear.

Blessed with love,
Beany found his mate.
Thankful for your help,
are Beany and Kate!

Our Thankful Bear

Two of them now but not for long. They're expecting a cub.

YEA! Let's sing a song!

"Joy to Beany and his one true love,
we sing and honor your special gift
from above.

Happy day! Happy day!

Time goes by, days and nights
the moment is here
the time is right.

Happy day! Happy day!

Beany and Kate had their cub.
His legs are sturdy, his smile so bright.
His name is Kurby.
He came through the night.

Happy day! Happy day!"

Beany's luck has changed completely.

Since a cub, so needy and young,
he now has Kate, who loves him deeply.

Your love and caring for this wee bear,
has paid off so dearly, with love to spare.

A family of three with friends all
around, has blessed their lives...

Because YOU were found!

Christine's heart cannot be limited to only
one genre.

She expresses her inspiration and imagination
through her books, poetry and sketches.

Christine aspires to keep on bringing us a
positive outlook on life through everything
she creates.

You can find Christine's inspiring
books through her

website: cloganinsideinspiration.com
or
email: tinemusic3@hotmail.com

About the Author

 Christine Logan's own experiences with making friends in her past and now, has always been easy for her.

In this book, she shows how easy, by reminding us it's a good way to live when we are accepting, kind and not judging those who are different than us.

She has been writing faithfully since 2011. Christine has self-published four books since then (including one she co-wrote with a former client, "Special Tribute to Mothers Everywhere").

Christine's most recent release "Suppose" was endorsed by a very talented author, H. W. Bryce, who wrote, "Chasing a Butterfly" in honour of his late wife.

Christine Logan has found her calling as a mother, wife, caregiver and as an author.

Christine lives in Maple Ridge, B.C. Canada with her husband and their loving two-year-old cat, "Snow White". Snow White shares her affections equally between them.

To find out more about Christine, please visit her
Website @ https://www.cloganinsideinspiration.com